CROSSWALK WALLY

STORY BY DAVE SHEA
ART BY PAT GILES

It was a really big day for Wally, because he and his bright yellow sign were headed to a brand new crosswalk at the corner of Main Street and Pine.

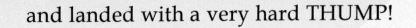

and landed with a very hard THUMP!

"Oh no!" said Wally as the truck drove away
toward the corner of Main Street and Pine,
"I don't know where I am or which way to go,
but I have to get back to my sign!"

"Perhaps I can help," said a kind, gentle voice.
"I can guide you to where you should be."
The voice came from a man on a little brown sign.
Wally asked, "And you'd do that for me?"

"It's my job," said the man on the little brown sign.
"It's what signs are supposed to do.
We help everyone safely find their way
and soon it will be your job, too."

"The corner you look for is just down the road,
but you must cross the street somewhere."
The man pointed the way toward a bright yellow sign.
"I think you can cross safely...right there."

Wally thanked the man for his kindness
and walked straight to the bright yellow sign.

"My name is Wally. Is this where I cross
to get to Main Street and Pine?"

"Sorry, Wally," said a voice from the sign,
"it's not safe for you to cross here.
Try the next sign. It's just down the road.
This crossing is only for deer."

Wally thanked the deer for its kindness and walked to the next yellow sign. "My name is Wally. Is this where I cross to get to Main Street and Pine?"

"Sorry Wally," said a voice from the sign,
"I'm afraid you're all out of luck.
Try the next sign. It's just down the road.
This crossing is only for ducks."

Wally thanked the duck for its kindness
and walked to the next several signs,

but none of them had a crosswalk
to get to Main Street and Pine.

He asked signs that said STOP
and signs that said SLOW.
He asked signs that had arrows
and signs that said NO.

"Sorry, Wally," they said all together,
"but that's not our job to do.
Try the next sign. It's just down the road.
Maybe that sign is for you."

Wally thanked them all for their kindness
and started to walk once again.
He thought, "I will never get across the street."

But all of a sudden…just then…

Wally spotted the sign they had mentioned
and what he saw he was happy to see.
"There are no words or animals on it," he said...

"Just a guy who looks just like me!"

Wally ran as fast as he possibly could
to the bottom of that bright yellow sign.
Looking up he shouted, "Excuse me, Sir,
is this the corner of Main Street and Pine?"

"It is," said the man who looked just like Wally.

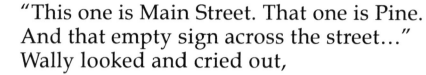

"This one is Main Street. That one is Pine.
And that empty sign across the street…"
Wally looked and cried out,

"Must be mine!"

"So, is this where I cross?
Can I safely cross here?"
Wally asked the crosswalk sign man.

He answered, "That's why I stand here.
That's what I do. To say, yes,
if you're careful, you can!"

So, Wally stepped to the edge of the sidewalk, looked both ways, not once, but two times.

When he was sure it was safe,
he carefully crossed.
Then up to the signpost he climbed!

Now Wally is back on his sign again,
in the rain and the snow and sunshine,
telling everyone there is a crosswalk
at the corner of Main Street and Pine.

Dave Shea is an advertising copywriter who has written hundreds of TV and radio commercials promoting everything from pre-sweetened cereals to luxury cars. He's a dad, grandfather, and a child at heart.

Pat Giles is an animator/cartoonist who has worked on many TV shows, web series, commercials, games, stickers and other fun pop-culture stuff. He is married to a YA novelist. They have two daughters and a pup named Sally. Ditto on "child at heart."

Made in United States
North Haven, CT
06 April 2022